The Jesus Bible

STUDY SERIES

PEOPLE

THE STORY OF GOD'S PROMISE

Aaron Coe, Ph.D.
Series Writer & General Editor of *The Jesus Bible*

Matt Rogers, Ph.D.
Series Writer & Lead Writer of *The Jesus Bible*

HarperChristian
Resources

passionpublishing

The Jesus Bible Study Series: People
© 2023 by Passion Publishing

Requests for information should be addressed to:
HarperChristian Resources, 3900 Sparks Dr. SE, Grand Rapids, Michigan 49546

ISBN 978-0-310-15502-7 (softcover)
ISBN 978-0-310-15503-4 (ebook)

HarperChristian Resources titles may be purchased in bulk for church, business, fundraising, or ministry use. For information, please e-mail ResourceSpecialist@ChurchSource.com.

First printing October 2023 / Printed in the United States of America

CONTENTS

INTRODUCTION

The Bible could have been a shorter collection of books were it not for God's radical grace. God's loving-kindness marked the dawn of creation. He created the world and all that is in it so that he would receive praise and worship from all that he made. From rocks to trees to the first man and woman, God intended everything to show off his greatness.

However, the beauty of his world changed when Adam and Eve disobeyed God and ate from the tree of the knowledge of good and evil. Adam and Eve willingly broke God's law because they doubted his goodness and failed to submit to his authority. We can picture the scene akin to a tranquil day lounging beside a quiet beach that transforms abruptly as a thunderstorm rolls in—from beauty to chaos in an instant. This is what took place in the Garden. But there was no passing storm, just the sinful choices of the first couple, and it changed everything.

One might assume that the rest of human history, and any subsequent stories throughout Scripture, would merely demonstrate God's hatred of evil and his coming judgment. But that is not what we find. In fact, hidden within the story of the Fall we find hints of God's mission to save sinners and fix the world. He promises that a Seed will come from Eve—a baby who will crush the head of Satan. He also enacts a plan to cover the sin of his people by killing an animal and literally covering the nakedness of Adam and Eve with the shed blood of another.

These themes weave throughout the Old Testament storyline, revealing just how God would bring these somewhat cryptic promises to fruition. From the story of the Fall in Genesis 3 forward, the Bible reveals the story of God's work to heal, restore, and save. Much later, the author of Hebrews, along with other New Testament writers, shows how these promises and patterns in the Old Testament help us understand the work of Jesus. This is the goal of this study. We will consider the working out of God's plan by focusing on the people he saves, most noticeably the nation of Israel. And we will identify several important themes found throughout the Old Testament and show how they all point forward to Jesus, who himself declared that all the Scriptures point to him testified to the things concerning himself (see Luke 24:27).

As a reminder, this is the third "act" in God's beautiful overarching story told throughout the Bible: (1) *Beginnings*, (2) *Revolt*, (3) *People*, (4) *Savior*, (5) *Church*, (6) *Forever*. Every detail in each story found within the pages of the Bible can be placed within one of these six acts, which tell God's story from Genesis to Revelation. This act, *People*, is vital for our understanding of God's mission because it reveals the Lord's response after his people rebelled against him. *People* also sets the stage for the coming acts—how we often try to "fix" the problem of our sin, as well as what God is going to do to right these wrongs through Jesus Christ.

Throughout *People*, we will navigate through dozens of books in the Bible, encapsulating hundreds of years of history. For this reason, you might want to work out the truths in *People* within the context of a Christian community. Note that at times, you will be asked to apply some aspect of God's story that you are reading to your own story through intentional reflection questions. So as you study *People*, we want to encourage you to come ready to engage your mind and your heart. Our prayer is that as you do, this study will push you to dig deeper into Scripture, help you discover God's truth for yourself, and come to understand the scope God's love to his *People*, shown through the person and work of Jesus Christ.

—Aaron & Matt

Lesson One

COVENANT

"The whole land of Canaan, where you now reside as a foreigner, I will give as an everlasting possession to you and your descendants after you; and I will be their God."

GENESIS 17:8

If you belong to Christ, then you are Abraham's seed, and heirs according to the promise.

GALATIANS 3:29

Let us hold unswervingly to the hope we profess, for he who promised is faithful.

— HEBREWS 10:23

WELCOME

Generally speaking, trust is built on track record. Your ability to trust others likely depends on how they have fulfilled their promises to you in the past. If someone has repeatedly let you down, then you probably won't give much credence to what they have to say. However, if someone comes through every time for you, then you most likely will trust them wholeheartedly.

We've all made promises. Some are small. "I'll pick up milk on the way home." "I'll get you that email in the morning." "I'll take the garbage cans out to the curb tonight." We keep some and break others. Broken promises at this level, while frustrating in the moment, aren't likely to amount to much more than a disappointed spouse or an irritated co-worker.

But then there are other kinds of promises that have a much greater impact when they are broken. For example, when a couple gets married, they traditionally say something like, "I take you to be my wedded wife/husband, to have and to hold from this day forward, for better, for worse, for richer, for poorer, in sickness and in health, to love and to cherish, till death do us part." This is a life-shifting promise that comes with far-reaching implications—both for the ones making the promise, as well as their children, friends, and extended family.

Keeping our promises is difficult because we're sinful beings living in a fallen world. We're frail and forgetful. We're prone to making compromises or cutting corners to make ourselves look better than we actually are. We give in to the gravitational pull of wickedness and undermine the words we speak with misaligned actions. The bottom line is we bail out on our promises far too often.

1. When is a time that someone broke a promise with you?

2. What impact did this broken promise have on you and on others?

READ

God's Call to Abram

In the previous study in this series, *Revolt*, we were introduced to a God who makes promises. The Lord pledged that a child of Eve would crush the head of the serpent—the enemy himself—and free the world of Satan, sin, and death (see Genesis 3:15). God is the one who made this promise, which should alert us to the magnitude of the claim. God said that he would prove victorious over sin and Satan because that is exactly what he promised to do in his Word.

Yet a cursory reading of the early chapters of Genesis might cause us to question if God will actually be true to his Word. Things seem to go from bad (Cain killing Abel in Genesis 4) to worse (an entire culture building a tower toward heaven so they could be like God in Genesis 11). Would God bail on his promises? Had the sin of the people finally gone too far? The answer is a resounding *no*! Instead, God was about to raise up a man whom he would bring into a special and personal relationship with himself, as the following passage relates:

> [1] *The Lord had said to Abram, "Go from your country, your people and your father's household to the land I will show you.*
>
> > [2] *"I will make you into a great nation,*
> > > *and I will bless you;*
> > *I will make your name great,*
> > > *and you will be a blessing.*
> > [3] *I will bless those who bless you,*
> > > *and whoever curses you I will curse;*
> > *and all peoples on earth*
> > > *will be blessed through you."*
>
> [4] *So Abram went, as the Lord had told him; and Lot went with him. Abram was seventy-five years old when he set out from Harran. [5] He took his wife Sarai, his nephew Lot, all the possessions they had accumulated and the people they had acquired in Harran, and they set out for the land of Canaan.*
>
> Genesis 12:1–5

We're told nothing of Abram (later renamed Abraham) up to this point, yet it is clear that God was aware of him and his family. As a demonstration of his grace, the Lord chose Abram to be the one through whom the promises of Genesis 3 would be realized. Abram would be the father of a people who would serve as a blessing to the nations, and through his line would come a plan that would cause "all peoples on earth" to be blessed. Even though Abram's wife, Sarai (later renamed Sarah), was barren, he chose to believe God's promises, and "[God] credited it to him as righteousness" (Genesis 15:6). This pattern serves as a foreshadowing of how all people would be saved—they would believe God's promises through faith.

3. Imagine the state of despair that people were in when God made this promise to Abram. How would the Lord's words in this passage have begun to shift their outlook?

4. List some of the promises that God made to Abram. How did Abram respond when he received this calling from the Lord?

An Elaborate Ceremony

God's next act was to conduct an elaborate ceremony to seal his promises with Abraham (see Genesis 15:9). The scene that followed would have been familiar to anyone living in the ancient Near East. In the ritual, slaughtered animals were placed on the opposite sides of a narrow path, their blood filling the walkway. The two parties involved in making the promise walked down the path of blood, signifying that if either of them failed to uphold their end of the promise, they should be killed as if they were the slaughtered animals. It was a vivid way to symbolize the significance of a commitment. Either the parties kept their word, or they died.

*⁹ So the L*ᴏʀᴅ *said to him, "Bring me a heifer, a goat and a ram, each three years old, along with a dove and a young pigeon."*

¹⁰ Abram brought all these to him, cut them in two and arranged the halves opposite each other; the birds, however, he did not cut in half. ¹¹ Then birds of prey came down on the carcasses, but Abram drove them away.

*¹² As the sun was setting, Abram fell into a deep sleep, and a thick and dreadful darkness came over him. ¹³ Then the L*ᴏʀᴅ *said to him, "Know for certain that for four hundred years your descendants will be strangers in a country not their own and that they will be enslaved and mistreated there. ¹⁴ But I will punish the nation they serve as slaves, and afterward they will come out with great possessions. ¹⁵ You, however, will go to your ancestors in peace and be buried at a good old age. ¹⁶ In the fourth generation your descendants will come back here, for the sin of the Amorites has not yet reached its full measure."*

¹⁷ When the sun had set and darkness had fallen, a smoking firepot with a blazing torch appeared and passed between the pieces.

Genesis 15:9–17

But notice that on this occasion, it was not God and Abram who walked down the blood path together. Instead, the Lord caused Abram to fall into a deep sleep, and then God walked the path *alone*. The smoking firepot and flaming torch were symbols of God's presence and showed that he was the one committing to keep his promises to Abraham. He did this knowing full well that Abraham and his children would not fully uphold their end of the deal—that they would fail to walk faithfully with him and keep his statutes and laws.

These scenes are among the first places the Bible uses the language of "covenant." The most common image in our culture of covenants takes place at a marriage ceremony. Marriage is not simply a legally binding contract but also a covenantal pledge between two parties to commit to loving one another. Today, the high proportion of marriages ending in divorce show the frailty of even the best of human covenants. Yet the fact that marriages fail does not undermine the nature of the promise in the first place. When couples pledge, "Till death do us part," that's exactly what they should be promising to one another. Upholding these commitments is a picture of the promise-keeping nature of God (see Ephesians 5:22–33).

Thankfully, the Bible's story isn't about the ability of people to keep their promises. Rather, it shows the faithfulness of God to keep his covenant promises. The hope of a covenant rests in the ability of the covenant makers to uphold their promises, and since the promise maker in the Bible is God, we can be certain that he will keep his promises, because he cannot lie. Abram would realize this when God reaffirmed his promises to him (see Genesis 17:1–8)

5. Imagine what it would have been like for Abram and Sarai to hear these promises from God for the first time. What doubts do you think they had?

6. Have you ever been in a position when someone made a promise that seemed too good to be true? If so, what happened, and how did you feel?

REFLECT

God Always Finds a Way

We've been trained to think of promises as too good to be true because, in a fallen world, they often are. People let us down and fail to keep their word. In the same way, we let people down and fail to keep our word. Broken promises often lead to more broken promises, as we cower in shame and guilt, knowing we haven't lived up to our standard or—more importantly—God's.

But God is different. He *always* keeps his promises. In fact, the story of the Bible testifies to God's faithfulness, even though it constantly seems that the odds are stacked against him. Even in the story of Abram and his descendants, we see that people are woefully incapable of keeping their word. Right after God's call, Abram traveled to Egypt to escape a famine, where he lied to protect himself and his family (see Genesis 12:10–20). His descendants (Jacob in particular) would follow in this pattern and lie, trick, and deceive others.

Further, the women in Abram's line are consistently barren. First Sarai, his wife, is unable to conceive. Then Rebekah, the wife of Abram's son Isaac, is childless. Then Rachel, the wife of Isaac's son Jacob, is also unable to bear children. All of this might cause us to wonder if God's promise of a coming Seed from Abram's line is going to end at any moment, as each generation hangs by a thread. Yet repeatedly, God gives hope and provides life where it was thought to be impossible. He proves that he is always faithful to his promises.

God continues to reiterate his covenantal promises to each of the patriarchs that follow after Abram: Isaac, Jacob, and then Joseph. Genesis actually culminates with the story of Joseph and reveals that God always keeps his promises in spite of the situation. Joseph is the youngest of Isaac's twelve sons and seems to be an unlikely choice for God's promise-keeping mission. But Joseph is just the kind of person God loves to use—the youngest, the weakest, the misfit, the broken. God's story shows that these are the instruments he uses to bring Jesus into this world—and the types of people he continues to use to this day.

In Joseph's case, his story gets worse before it gets better. He is sold into slavery by his brothers and taken to Egypt, where he ends up a slave in the home of Potiphar, the captain of the guard. He is unfairly jailed after a false accusation by Potiphar's wife, who feels spurned when Joseph resists her advances. While in prison, he is forgotten by a fellow prisoner who could have put in a good word for him in Pharaoh's court. It all seems hopeless at times for Joseph, but God ultimately reveals that he can even work through things that people intend for evil to bring about his good purposes (see Genesis 50:20). This includes his promises for the salvation of the nation of Israel—those who inherit God's promises from Genesis 12.

7. When has God used what others intended for evil to bring about something good in your life?

8. How did you feel when you didn't know the outcome of what that situation would be? How do you feel now that you can look back and see evidence of God's faithfulness?

Drenched in God's Faithfulness

Our lives, whether we recognize it or not, are drenched with the faithfulness of God. Sadly, it often requires turmoil or hardships to make us aware of this reality. Our lives are broken by pain. We doubt God and fear that he has abandoned us. We wonder how we can go on. But faced with all these fears, God calls us to remember his promises and his faithful character:

The LORD your God is God; he is the faithful God, keeping his covenant of love to a thousand generations of those who love him and keep his commandments.

Deuteronomy 7:9

He will cover you with his feathers, and under his wings you will find refuge; his faithfulness will be your shield and rampart.

Psalm 91:4

If we are faithless, he remains faithful, for he cannot disown himself.

2 Timothy 2:13

Let us hold unswervingly to the hope we profess, for he who promised is faithful.

Hebrews 10:23

These magnificent promises give us hope in a world that is torn apart by unkept promises. But know this: God is always faithful. He will not abandon us. His love is strong. He is not like the people in our lives who have broken their promises. He demonstrates that he is perfect by perfectly keeping his word. Yet it must be asked: *To whom do these promises apply?* The answer is clear: God's people. God pledges his covenant love to all his people who have placed their faith in him and experienced the new life that Jesus brings.

Paul makes this point evident when he writes, "If you belong to Christ, then you are Abraham's seed, and heirs according to the promise" (Galatians 3:29). The promises of God now extend beyond the boundaries of ancient Israel. All people—regardless of ethnicity, background, socio-economic status, or any other worldly dividing line—can inherit the promises that God made to Abraham. They can know God as their God and experience the joy of being his people. The New Testament writers help us understand the way that all these promises from God are now fulfilled in the church, but one thing is crystal clear: those who belong to Christ can live with rock-solid confidence and trust in God.

Not only that, but the offer of hope in God's promises extends to those who have not yet placed their faith in Jesus Christ. They, too, can turn from their sins and be saved, knowing this truth: "If we confess our sins, he is faithful and just and will forgive us our sins and purify us from all unrighteousness" (1 John 1:9). There, again, we see the faithfulness of God on display. He promises to forgive those who come to him and confess their sins.

9. What are some moments of hardship in your life that God used to reveal his faithfulness to you? What did you learn about him through the experience?

10. What impact does it have on you to know that you are a part of God's people?

CLOSE

In the end, it doesn't matter what our background is or the mistakes that we have made in our past. God stands ready and willing to forgive and restore *anyone* who asks. This offer of forgiveness from a faithful God extends to us all. We, who were once estranged from God, can now become "his people" in Jesus Christ.

11. Why do you think that it is often so tempting to doubt God's ability to keep his promises?

12. How should the reality of God's faithfulness shape the way that you live?

Lesson Two

THE LAW

*"I am the LORD your God, who brought you out of Egypt,
out of the land of slavery."*

EXODUS 20:2

*So then, the law is holy, and the commandment is holy,
righteous and good.*

ROMANS 7:12

This is love for God:

to keep his commands.

And his commands

are not burdensome.

— 1 JOHN 5:3

WELCOME

Anyone who's driven on an interstate understands the role of lane markers. The dashed white lines alert you to know when you are leaving your lane and switching into another. Crossing that marker, if done appropriately, is the way the road was designed. But solid lines, rumble strips, and medians are not intended to be crossed—and when a driver does cross them, the consequences can be dire. When everyone adheres to the markers on the road the way they were intended, we are all more likely to arrive at our destinations safely and efficiently.

The intent of lane markers—alerting us to what is safe to cross or when we need to stay in our lane—is for our collective good as drivers. In the same way, rules, when built on the truth of God's Word, are designed for our good as human beings. They tell us when it is safe and permissible to do certain things and when we should just stay in our "lane." God's rules create pathways to flourishing.

The rules that God gave to Abraham's descendants reflected the outworking of his faithful character and were intended to help them flourish as a people. However, by the time we pick up their story in Exodus, it seems that Abraham's descendants—the nation of Israel—were far away from where they should have been. We could say they had crossed a few solid lane markers, moving from the land of Canaan in

Joseph's day to escape a famine . . . and remained there. Now they were enslaved in Egypt—trapped under the harsh yoke of a pagan nation.

1. What is a rule that you do not like but know it is for your good?

2. What has happened when you have broken that rule?

READ

God Raises Up a Leader

However, God wasn't about to turn his back on the Israelites. Ever faithful, he was about to raise up a man to lead them and orchestrate their miraculous deliverance. But first, the Lord had to convince this man that he was the right person for the job.

> [7] The LORD said, "I have indeed seen the misery of my people in Egypt. I have heard them crying out because of their slave drivers, and I am concerned about their suffering. [8] So I have come down to rescue them from the hand of the Egyptians and to bring them up out of that land into a good and spacious land, a land flowing with milk and honey—the home of the Canaanites,

Hittites, Amorites, Perizzites, Hivites and Jebusites. ⁹ And now the cry of the Israelites has reached me, and I have seen the way the Egyptians are oppressing them. ¹⁰ So now, go. I am sending you to Pharaoh to bring my people the Israelites out of Egypt."

¹¹ But Moses said to God, "Who am I that I should go to Pharaoh and bring the Israelites out of Egypt?"

¹² And God said, "I will be with you. And this will be the sign to you that it is I who have sent you: When you have brought the people out of Egypt, you will worship God on this mountain."

¹³ Moses said to God, "Suppose I go to the Israelites and say to them, 'The God of your fathers has sent me to you,' and they ask me, 'What is his name?' Then what shall I tell them?"

¹⁴ God said to Moses, "I AM WHO I AM. This is what you are to say to the Israelites: 'I AM has sent me to you.'"

Exodus 3:7–14

In spite of Moses' hesitations, he eventually did what God instructed him to do and confronted Pharoah, telling him to let the Lord's people go. When Pharaoh refused, God unleashed a series of ten plagues on Egypt, culminating in the death of the firstborn in any home that did not have the blood of a sacrificial lamb on their doorpost. Pharaoh finally relented and the Israelites quickly fled in the middle of the night, but then Pharaoh changed his mind. He hurried his army out to intercept the fleeing Israelites and caught up with them at the Red Sea. Stuck between a sea and the Egyptian army, it looked as if the Israelites were trapped. But God parted the waters of the Red Sea and led them safely through on dry land. When the Egyptians tried to pursue, God closed the waters and washed them away.

God had freed his people from slavery as a demonstration of his faithfulness. The miracles that follow in the book of Exodus are not happenstance. Rather, they are done to show that God is glorious and has the power over nature and the ability to do anything he wants. The Exodus proved to the Israelites that God had not abandoned them, even though they continued to sin against him. He didn't measure out his grace and kindness the way that we often do. When people wrong us, we tend to lash out or get even, but God doesn't act that way because he is holy. He bases all of his actions on his faithful character and his perfect plan. This was meant to provoke the people who experienced his grace to worship him whole-heartedly.

3. What does God say to Moses that he had seen about the Israelites' situation?

4. How did God prove through the events of the Exodus that he had kept his promises to his people?

A Call to Keep God's Covenant

A short time later, God led his people though the wilderness to the foot of Mount Sinai. There the Lord called them to keep his covenant—which, in this context, meant they were to live like his people. They were to strive to obey him because of his grace in their lives. It is clear at this point that God had special intentions for the nation of Israel. Among all the people groups in the world, God chose the Israelites to be his—his treasured possession, his kingdom of priests, his holy nation—and so he gave them a set of laws to help them "stay in their lane." Far from an unreasonable set of commands, these identity markers were intended as a great privilege.

[1]*And God spoke all these words:*

[2] *"I am the L*ORD *your God, who brought you out of Egypt, out of the land of slavery.*

[3] *"You shall have no other gods before me.*

[4] *"You shall not make for yourself an image in the form of anything in heaven above or on the earth beneath or in the waters below.* [5] *You shall not bow down to them or worship them; for I, the L*ORD *your God, am a jealous God, punishing the children for the sin of the parents to the third and fourth generation of those who hate me,* [6] *but showing love to a thousand generations of those who love me and keep my commandments.*

[7] *"You shall not misuse the name of the L*ORD *your God, for the L*ORD *will not hold anyone guiltless who misuses his name.*

[8] *"Remember the Sabbath day by keeping it holy.* [9] *Six days you shall labor and do all your work,* [10] *but the seventh day is a sabbath to the L*ORD *your God. On it you shall not do any work, neither you, nor your son or daughter, nor your male or female servant, nor your animals, nor any foreigner residing in your towns.* [11] *For in six days the L*ORD *made the heavens and the earth, the sea, and all that is in them, but he rested on the seventh day. Therefore the L*ORD *blessed the Sabbath day and made it holy.*

[12] *"Honor your father and your mother, so that you may live long in the land the L*ORD *your God is giving you.*

[13] *"You shall not murder.*

[14] *"You shall not commit adultery.*

[15] *"You shall not steal.*

[16] *"You shall not give false testimony against your neighbor.*

[17] *"You shall not covet your neighbor's house. You shall not covet your neighbor's wife, or his male or female servant, his ox or donkey, or anything that belongs to your neighbor."*

[18] *When the people saw the thunder and lightning and heard the trumpet and saw the mountain in smoke, they trembled with fear. They stayed at a distance* [19] *and said to Moses, "Speak to us yourself and we will listen. But do not have God speak to us or we will die."*

[20] *Moses said to the people, "Do not be afraid. God has come to test you, so that the fear of God will be with you to keep you from sinning."*

[21] *The people remained at a distance, while Moses approached the thick darkness where God was.*

Exodus 20:1-21

The context in which Moses received the Ten Commandments on Mount Sinai was the joyful privilege of getting to be God's possession. In reality, the Ten Commandments would be but a small percentage of the host of other laws that God gave to his people throughout the latter half of the book of Exodus. God defined for his people what it meant to live in light of his promises. He described how they should behave as a chosen, beloved people. It was not a laundry list of commands that Israel had to fulfill in order to merit God's love. They had already experienced his love. Now they were to obey his commands as a way to worship him.

5. How are the Ten Commandments a picture of the faithfulness of God?

6. What are some ways these commandments are a blessing to God's people?

Promises Shape Priorities

Many have pointed out that the Ten Commandments can be categorized in two parts. The first four Commandments inform the people's love for God, while the next six describe the relationships they were to have with one another. The other 600-plus laws recorded in the chapters that follow outline how to worship God, live in harmony with one another, and maintain purity in their lives. Because these laws were given to ancient Israel, there are some that are unique to their role in God's mission and the unique time and context in which they lived. Others are later reinforced by Jesus in the New Testament and apply to all people.

God gave the law so his people would know how to model his character through worshipful obedience. Looking back to Genesis 1, God created men and women, and then he gave them the task of filling the earth with image-bearing worshipers (see Genesis 1:26–28). If Adam and Eve modeled the character of God through holy living, they were positioned to accomplish their task of portraying him to the world. In many ways people are intended to be a mirror, taking in the image of God and then tilting outward to reflect that image to the watching world.

Should Israel have been faithful to the law, they would have painted a picture for the watching world of what God's people looked like. Writing many years later, the prophet Isaiah claimed this was God's intention for Israel: "I will make you [Israel] as a light for the nations, that my salvation may reach to the end of the earth" (Isaiah 49:6). While Israel was God's chosen people, they were designed to show off the character of God so the other nations would be drawn to worship him alongside them. The surrounding nations could look in on the nation of Israel and say, "Oh, so that's what people who've experienced God's grace look like."

Jesus picked up this theme when he said that those who follow him are "the light of the world" (Matthew 5:14). As God's people today, we have a similar mission as the nation of Israel in that we are called to paint a picture to the world of what God is like through our obedience. When we keep God's promises, we illustrate God's faithfulness. When we confess our sins, we show God's forgiveness. When we refrain from gossip, hatred, or sexual immorality, we show God's holiness. Christians mirror God to the world, which is what makes our hypocrisy so deadly. If we who wear the name of Christ do not accurately reflect his image to the world and keep his laws, we paint a false picture of God's character, as Paul notes in this passage:

> *7 What shall we say, then? Is the law sinful? Certainly not! Nevertheless, I would not have known what sin was had it not been for the law. For I would not have known what coveting really was if the law had not said, "You shall not covet." 8 But sin, seizing the opportunity afforded by the commandment, produced in me every kind of coveting. For apart from the law, sin was dead. 9 Once I was alive apart from the law; but when the commandment came, sin sprang to life and I died. 10 I found that the very commandment that was intended to bring life actually brought death. 11 For sin, seizing the opportunity afforded by the commandment, deceived me, and through the commandment put me to death. 12 So then, the law is holy, and the commandment is holy, righteous and good.*
>
> Romans 7:7-12

7.   What does Paul say that God's laws reveal to us?

8. What are some of the blessings the law brings to us?

REFLECT

Most people want to push back on rules. We live in a world that rejects authority and relentlessly strives to live in autonomy. No one likes to be told what to do. But God's laws are different. When we follow God's rules, it enables us to do what he originally created us to do—reflect his image to the world. Further, because God always wants the best for us, following his rules lead to us getting the best things that he has for us in this life. We may think of God's rules as being restrictive, but they actually lead to joy, peace, and contentment. Following God's rules also gives us freedom, for following our own rules ultimately only leads to bondage and sin (see Psalm 1).

We are meant to live under authority for our own good. Anyone who has ever parented a child knows this reality. Infants and toddlers are incapable of functioning on their own. They literally cannot survive without a caregiver structuring their lives with appropriate boundaries. Caregivers keep young children out of the road and away from knives in the cabinet. They set appropriate boundaries as their children age. A loving father establishes parameters of how, when, and who his daughter dates. A wise mother expects her son to be home by curfew. These commands are not arbitrary but allow the one under authority to thrive.

It is difficult for most of us to believe that authority is for our good because we've seen authority abused time and time again. We've seen people in positions of power take advantage of others in a way that has caused lasting pain. Yet we must reject the association of human authority with God's authority. God does not take advantage of his power. He does not subjugate people to harsh rules. He is not out to crush us. Again, he simply wants us to live under his authority because he knows it is for our good.

In fact, this was the intention in the Garden of Eden. Adam and Eve were created to submit to God's authority because he knew what was best for them. He knew what the consequences would be if they ate the fruit of the tree that he had told them to avoid. The chaos that resulted from Adam and Eve's choice was no surprise to God. While the command to avoid the fruit must have seemed arbitrary to them, it was a rule, a boundary, that was put in place to protect them. God's rules were—and are—a demonstration of his love.

9. When words like *authority*, *rules*, or *laws* are mentioned, what comes to mind for you?

10. What evidence do you have that God's ways are better than your ways and that he always knows what is best for you?

CLOSE

God makes rules because he loves his people. He wants what is best for us. When-ever we are tempted to rebel from God's authority, we need to retrain our minds to believe that he knows how life is meant to be lived. When Paul writes that we are to offer our bodies as a living sacrifice to God, he says that the way we do this is by renewing our minds (see Romans 12:1–2). We have to retrain our minds to believe that God's purposes and plans are better than what our eyes can see and our minds can understand. When we do this, we acknowledge that God is better at being in charge of our lives than we are under our own authority.

11. What does it mean to offer your body to God as a living sacrifice? Why is sac-rifice a necessary part of submitting your will to God's?

12. What are some of the ways that you see God renewing your mind day by day?

Lesson Three

WORSHIP

*But Moses sought the favor of the L*ORD *his God. "L*ORD*," he said, "why should your anger burn against your people, whom you brought out of Egypt with great power and a mighty hand?"*

EXODUS 32:11

For this reason Christ is the mediator of a new covenant, that those who are called may receive the promised eternal inheritance—now that he has died as a ransom to set them free from the sins committed under the first covenant.

HEBREWS 9:15

Come, let us bow
down in worship,
let us kneel before the
Lᴏʀᴅ our Maker.

— PSALM 95:6

WELCOME

My (Aaron's) wife, Carmen, and I have been married for more than twenty-five years. We actually met each other when we were in the sixth grade. This means that as write this, we have known each other for more than three-quarters of our lives. In that time, we have been through our share of ups and some downs. We have added four amazing children to our family—two adopted and two biological. We lead very full lives.

Like all marriages, ours takes work. After all, two people don't stick together as long as we have without being intentional about the relationship. I would say that one of the keys to our longevity has been that we have been quick to forgive each other. When we have wronged each other, we have refused to live in that struggle for very long.

But even the best relationships can go sideways fairly easily. A person says something that offends his or her friend, and pretty soon cold shoulders and harsh words are the norm. College roommates who thought they would be friends forever allow the pressures and the pace of life to pull them apart. A husband and wife fail to confess sin and ask for forgiveness, and soon the marriage is filled with fury—sometimes stated, but oftentimes hidden, behind a veil of unspoken resentment.

Broken relationships are evidence of the Fall that occurred in the Garden of Eden when Adam and Eve chose to break God's law. The Lord intended people to live in community with one another, marked by peace, respect, and mutual care. Marriages, families, and friendships should be places of safety and confident love. But the sin in the Garden changed all that. Now all human relationships, even the best ones, are marked by the evidence of sin's impact.

1. What is an example in your life of a relationship that was (or is) broken?

2. What has been the impact of that broken relationship on your life?

READ

Marred by Sin

But even more, broken human relationships are indicative of a more fundamental relationship that was broken—that between humans and God. Again, this was not God's original design. He created people out of love. God wanted to be known and experience the intimacy of worship from his created image-bearers. Human sin changed all this. People were now marred by sin, which meant that a holy God could not experience intimacy with them the way that he intended.

That is, he couldn't unless something changed. And for something to change, God would have to be the one to make the change, because people proved to be incapable of breaking their slavery to sin. This story from Exodus reveals the sad state of affairs among his people:

> *¹When the people saw that Moses was so long in coming down from the mountain, they gathered around Aaron and said, "Come, make us gods who*

will go before us. As for this fellow Moses who brought us up out of Egypt, we don't know what has happened to him."

² Aaron answered them, "Take off the gold earrings that your wives, your sons and your daughters are wearing, and bring them to me." ³ So all the people took off their earrings and brought them to Aaron. ⁴ He took what they handed him and made it into an idol cast in the shape of a calf, fashioning it with a tool. Then they said, "These are your gods, Israel, who brought you up out of Egypt."

⁵ When Aaron saw this, he built an altar in front of the calf and announced, "Tomorrow there will be a festival to the Lord." ⁶ So the next day the people rose early and sacrificed burnt offerings and presented fellowship offerings. Afterward they sat down to eat and drink and got up to indulge in revelry.

⁷ Then the Lord said to Moses, "Go down, because your people, whom you brought up out of Egypt, have become corrupt. ⁸ They have been quick to turn away from what I commanded them and have made themselves an idol cast in the shape of a calf. They have bowed down to it and sacrificed to it and have said, 'These are your gods, Israel, who brought you up out of Egypt.'

⁹ "I have seen these people," the Lord said to Moses, "and they are a stiff-necked people. ¹⁰ Now leave me alone so that my anger may burn against them and that I may destroy them. Then I will make you into a great nation."

¹¹ But Moses sought the favor of the Lord his God. "Lord," he said, "why should your anger burn against your people, whom you brought out of Egypt with great power and a mighty hand? ¹² Why should the Egyptians say, 'It was with evil intent that he brought them out, to kill them in the mountains and to wipe them off the face of the earth'? Turn from your fierce anger; relent and do not bring disaster on your people. ¹³ Remember your servants Abraham, Isaac and Israel, to whom you swore by your own self: 'I will make your descendants as numerous as the stars in the sky and I will give your descendants all this land I promised them, and it will be their inheritance forever.'" ¹⁴ Then the Lord relented and did not bring on his people the disaster he had threatened.

Exodus 32:1–14

Moses was receiving the law of the Lord—and the people were already breaking that law. They doubted God's leadership and wondered what was taking Moses so long. So, what did the Israelites do? They made a god for themselves. Seriously, it would be comical if it weren't so sad. These were the same people who had just witnessed God part the Red Sea and crush the most powerful nation in the world. They had every reason to trust God. But they didn't. These sinful people, trapped in a cycle of rebellion against God, could not worship and love the Lord the way they were created to do. They were estranged from him—separated because of their rebellion.

3. The Israelites had seen God part the Red Sea and crush the Egyptian army. So why did they so quickly doubt God when Moses didn't come down the mountain right away?

4. What did God decide to do against the Israelites in this situation? What did Moses say to persuade the Lord to do otherwise?

The Path Back to God

The Israelites' only hope was for God to intervene and restore his relationship with them. The imagery throughout the later portion of Exodus and into Leviticus is meant to demonstrate how God orchestrates this. A word of warning at this point: This portion of the Bible can be notoriously difficult to understand and apply. It is easy for the reader to get lost in the weeds. So, for our purposes, we will consider three themes that help us understand how God made it possible for sinful people to have a relationship with him: (1) the tabernacle, (2) the sacrificial system, and (3) the priests.

First, God instructed Moses to build a tabernacle. The people were to give money and resources so that skillful builders could construct an elaborate tent according to God's exact specifications. The conclusion of the book of Exodus describes God's motive when, after the people finished its construction, "the cloud covered the tent of meeting, and the glory of the Lord filled the tabernacle" (Exodus 40:34). The tabernacle was a home for God's glory. God could not dwell in the midst of people because they were too sinful, so he set aside a space where his glory would dwell and where sinful people could approach him.

> [4] Moses said to the whole Israelite community, "This is what the Lord has commanded: [5] From what you have, take an offering for the Lord. Everyone who is willing is to bring to the Lord an offering of gold, silver and bronze; [6] blue, purple and scarlet yarn and fine linen; goat hair; [7] ram skins dyed red and another type of durable leather; acacia wood; [8] olive oil for the light; spices for the anointing oil and for the fragrant incense; [9] and onyx stones and other gems to be mounted on the ephod and breastpiece.
>
> [10] "All who are skilled among you are to come and make everything the Lord has commanded: [11] the tabernacle with its tent and its covering, clasps, frames, crossbars, posts and bases; [12] the ark with its poles and the atonement cover and the curtain that shields it; [13] the table with its poles and all its articles and the bread of the Presence; [14] the lampstand that is for light with its accessories, lamps and oil for the light; [15] the altar of incense with its poles, the anointing oil and the fragrant incense; the curtain for the doorway at the entrance to the tabernacle; [16] the altar of burnt offering with its bronze grating, its poles and all its utensils; the bronze basin with its stand; [17] the curtains of the courtyard with its posts and bases, and the curtain for the entrance to the courtyard; [18] the tent pegs for the tabernacle and for the courtyard, and their ropes; [19] the woven garments worn for ministering in the sanctuary—both the sacred garments for Aaron the priest and the garments for his sons when they serve as priests."

Exodus 35:4–19

Second, God established a sacrifical system. The tabernacle itself was not enough. Sinful people could not merely saunter into the presence of a holy God in any way that they wanted. The sacrificial system that God created allowed these sinful people to approach him in his chosen dwelling place. While there were different types of sacrifices and different reasons as to why the people would offer a sacrifice, the sin offering provides the most vivid picture of overall process.

> [27] *"'If any member of the community sins unintentionally and does what is forbidden in any of the Lord's commands, when they realize their guilt* [28] *and the sin they have committed becomes known, they must bring as their offering for the sin they committed a female goat without defect.* [29] *They are to lay their hand on the head of the sin offering and slaughter it at the place of the burnt offering.* [30] *Then the priest is to take some of the blood with his finger and put it on the horns of the altar of burnt offering and pour out the rest of the blood at the base of the altar.* [31] *They shall remove all the fat, just as the fat is removed from the fellowship offering, and the priest shall burn it on the altar as an aroma pleasing to the Lord. In this way the priest will make atonement for them, and they will be forgiven.'"*
>
> Leviticus 4:27–31

Third, the Lord set aside Aaron and his sons to serve as priests. (Aaron and his sons were of the tribe of Levi, one of the sons of Jacob, so it is also common to hear or read in Scripture of the Levitical priesthood.) As modern-day readers, we hear the word "priest" and immediately think of the current usage of the term, particularly within Catholicism. But the form the term takes today is a far cry from the original intention of the priesthood.

> [1] *The Lord said to Moses,* [2] *"Bring Aaron and his sons, their garments, the anointing oil, the bull for the sin offering, the two rams and the basket containing bread made without yeast,* [3] *and gather the entire assembly at the entrance to the tent of meeting."* [4] *Moses did as the Lord commanded him, and the assembly gathered at the entrance to the tent of meeting.*
>
> [5] *Moses said to the assembly, "This is what the Lord has commanded to be done."* [6] *Then Moses brought Aaron and his sons forward and washed them*

with water. ⁷ He put the tunic on Aaron, tied the sash around him, clothed him with the robe and put the ephod on him. He also fastened the ephod with a decorative waistband, which he tied around him. ⁸ He placed the breastpiece on him and put the Urim and Thummim in the breastpiece. ⁹ Then he placed the turban on Aaron's head and set the gold plate, the sacred emblem, on the front of it, as the LORD commanded Moses.

Leviticus 8:1–9

In the Old Testament, priests served as the representatives between God and his people. They were allowed access into the inner recesses of the temple, where they offered the sacrifices on behalf of the people. The priest would first place his hands on the sacrificial animal and confess the sins of the people—an image meant to show that the sins of the people were placed on the animal. Then the priest killed the animal and disposed of its limbs and organs in the way that had been specified by God. Most important, the priest then took the blood of the animal and poured it out on the altar of worship. The symbolism was clear—the blood covered the sin of the people as it covered the altar. Those whose sins had been forgiven through the blood sacrifice of another could now worship the Lord God as they should.

The priesthood was not glamorous; it was revolting. Each day was spent immersed in blood and animal carcasses. You can imagine the gory reality of blood-splattered clothes and the smells of death wafting through the air. The reality of death would leave no mistake in the minds of the priests or the average Israelite: *sin was a big deal.*

5. Imagine you lived in Israel during the time of the tabernacle, sacrificial system, and priesthood. What do you think you would have thought about sin?

6. What would you have understood to be true of God?

A Substitute for the Penalty

The path to God was paved with blood. The graphic description of the sacrificial animals was meant to evoke a visceral reaction from the people. They would understand, as Paul would later write, that "the wages of sin is death" (Romans 6:23). But this begs the question: It was not the animals that had sinned and deserved to die—so why all the animal carcasses? The answer can be found back in the Garden of Eden after Adam and Eve sinned:

> *21 The LORD God made garments of skin for Adam and his wife and clothed them. 22 And the LORD God said, "The man has now become like one of us, knowing good and evil. He must not be allowed to reach out his hand and take also from the tree of life and eat, and live forever." 23 So the LORD God banished him from the Garden of Eden to work the ground from which he had been taken. 24 After he drove the man out, he placed on the east side of the Garden of Eden cherubim and a flaming sword flashing back and forth to guard the way to the tree of life.*
>
> Genesis 3:21–24

In this scene, Adam and Eve had just received the consequences from God for their sinful disobedience of eating from the tree of the knowledge of good and evil. They hid behind fig leaves to cover their shame. God, however, had another plan. He made garments of animal skins to clothe them. God made the first animal sacrifice, not for himself, but on behalf of Adam and Eve. Something else died so that Adam and Eve could continue to live.

It was a substitute—someone, or something, who takes the place of someone else and receives the benefits or consequences the other deserves. Sinful people deserve death, so an animal dies in their place as a substitute. This makes it possible for them to be forgiven because the substitute has paid their penalty. This process is the way God could be just and judge sin yet still show mercy and grace by allowing his people to live and worship. The image of sacrifice was clear—either the person dies or something (or someone) dies in his or her place.

7. Why is a substitute for sin necessary for you to be forgiven?

8. What would be the result if a substitute did not stand in for your sin?

REFLECT

God understood how difficult it would be to connect the dots between these ancient patterns of worship in the Old Testament and our lives today. One entire New Testament book is largely devoted to helping us grapple with how these dominant themes relate to Jesus—the book of Hebrews. This book can be summed up in one word: *better!* The author holds up many of the people and themes of the Old Testament and shows how Jesus is better.

For example, in Hebrews 5:1–10, the author says that Jesus is a better priest for the people because the Old Testament priests were sinners and had to make sacrifices for their own sins and the sins of the people. But not so with Jesus. He did not have to sacrifice for his sin because his was sinless. Also, the priests in the Old Testament died, so their office was not permanent. They had to be replaced, but Jesus lives and reigns forever (see Hebrews 7:26–28).

In Hebrews 9:11–28, the writer shows that Jesus is a better sacrificial offering because he offered himself up, once and for all, for the sins of his people. Similar to the Old

Testament sacrifices, the blood of a substitute covered human sin—but now it was the blood of the very Son of God. It was no longer necessary for an endless stream of dead animals to substitute for human sin because the true Lamb of God had now taken away the sins of the world (see John 1:29). Priests were no longer needed to stand in the tabernacle or temple and offer sacrifices, since Jesus, as the perfect priest and sacrifice, had finished the work and sat down from his labors, symbolizing the perfect completion of his task. The conclusion? "For by a single offering he has perfected for all time those who are being sanctified" (Hebrews 10:14 ESV).

And what about the tabernacle? John's Gospel opens with an allusion to this theme when he writes, "The Word [Jesus] became flesh and made his dwelling among us. We have seen his glory, the glory of the one and only Son, who came from the Father, full of grace and truth" (John 1:14). The word *dwell* in this verse is a picture of the tabernacle—the place where God's glory dwelled among the ancient Israelites. Now, through Jesus, this dwelling would not be in a building made by human hands but in a person, the Lord Jesus Christ. He would dwell in our world as the perfect Son of God, embodying all of God's glory.

9. According to the author of Hebrews, what are some of the reasons why Jesus is the better priest and sacrificial offering for his people?

10. How does the Old Testament tabernacle, the sacrificial system, and the priesthood help you understand Jesus better?

CLOSE

Not only do these images help us better understand Jesus, but they also paint a picture for us of the lives we are meant to live as Christ-followers. As noted previously, Paul in Romans 12:1–2 asserts that Christians are to offer their lives as a living sacrifice to God. Jesus says that his people must die to themselves in order to live for him (see Mark 8:34–35). Because of Jesus' sacrifice and the forgiveness he offers, God's people then sacrifice their lives, both literally and figuratively, in order to follow him. For some, this literally means giving up their lives as martyrs for the cause of Christ around the world. But for most of us, it means being willing to give up our dreams, aspirations, resources, and gifts so that Jesus' name will be known and worshiped.

11. What steps has God taken to restore a right relationship with sinful people?

12. What has this lesson revealed to you about what it means to worship God?

Lesson Four

LAND

"I will be with you and will bless you. For to you and your descendants I will give all these lands and will confirm the oath I swore to your father Abraham."

GENESIS 26:3

"But what about you?" he asked. "Who do you say I am?"

MATTHEW 16:15

The land is mine
and you reside
in my land as foreigners
and strangers.

— LEVITICUS 25:23

WELCOME

There are certain places—cities, houses, vacation destinations—that conjure up images in our minds. We've spent moments in these locations that have shaped the people we are today. For some of us, it's the home we grew up in as a child, where we built forts in the woods or learned to ride a bike or played endless games with friends in the front yard. Many of us can remember the floor-plan of this home, and the very sight of the old house floods our hearts with emotion. Places are special, even if the place itself is ordinary.

Places are often significant in God's story as well. Sometimes in Scripture, the place simply serves as a backdrop to a story, but in many cases, the place is actually the point of the story. As we've previously seen, God gave the Israelites the law at a special place—Mount Sinai. He dwelt with his people in an intricately crafted place—the tabernacle. These places would forever shape the memories of the Israelites, yet they were not the place they longed for most.

1. What are some places that have special memories attached to them for you?

2. What is it about these places that make them special?

READ

The Place Is the Point

When God appeared to Abraham and promised to make him "into a great nation" (Genesis 12:2), he led him from his home country into a place that he did not know. Sometime later, the Lord again appeared to Abraham and promised to give him and his descendants that special place. God said, "I am the LORD, who brought you out of Ur of the Chaldeans to give you this land to take possession of it" (15:7). This land was a promise that God made to Abraham, so it became known as the "Promised Land," though it was also called Canaan. Later, the Lord would reiterate this same promise to Isaac, the son of Abraham and Sarah:

> [1] *Now there was a famine in the land—besides the previous famine in Abraham's time—and Isaac went to Abimelek king of the Philistines in Gerar.* [2] *The LORD appeared to Isaac and said, "Do not go down to Egypt; live in the land where I tell you to live.* [3] *Stay in this land for a while, and I will be with you and will bless you. For to you and your descendants I will give all these lands and will confirm the oath I swore to your father Abraham.* [4] *I will make your descendants as numerous as the stars in the sky and will give them all these lands, and through your offspring all nations on earth will be blessed,* [5] *because Abraham obeyed me and did everything I required of him, keeping my commands, my decrees and my instructions."* [6] *So Isaac stayed in Gerar.*

> Genesis 26:1–6

The Israelites' 430-year stint as slaves in Egypt heightened their longing for a land to call their home. So, once the Lord freed them from Egyptian bondage, the nation moved toward the Promised Land by way of Mount Sinai. This place where God was leading his people was not just any land. It wasn't a remote patch of territory that no one else wanted. It was prime real estate—a land that would soon be the epicenter of the known world.

3. Put yourself into the place of the ancient Israelites. What would you have looked forward to the most about the Promised Land?

4. Why would the thought of the Promised Land bring up strong emotions?

A Good, Spacious, and Luxurious Land

Before the Exodus, God had described this land to Moses as "a good and spacious land, a land flowing with milk and honey" (Exodus 3:8; see also verse 17). Three descriptions are worthy of note. First, it was a good land. Now, when you and I say the word *good*, we are likely implying that something is just better than average. Not so with God. Remember, when God looked on the world he created—the heavens, the earth, the rivers, the mountains, the animals, and all of it—he declared that it was good (see Genesis 1:4, 9, 12, 18, 21, 25, 31). When God says something is good, we can rest assured that he means it is special indeed.

Not only was the land good, but it was also spacious. In the ancient Near East, such a description implied that the territory was sufficient to meet the needs of a society that lived off it. In the Israelites' case, spacious land would have been required, as it needed to hold at least two million people plus all their livestock. This type of land would hold out hope for each member of society to have a place to call home and make his or her own.

Finally, and most vividly, the land was flowing with milk and honey. It is certain that both these terms *milk* and *honey* are used here as descriptors of luxury. They were the best of the best—all the good things in life. The Promised Land would be fertile, causing it to flow with bountiful provision. The language here brings to mind the original Garden of Eden, a lush paradise meant to be enjoyed. The land didn't simply just have milk and honey, but it flowed with luxuries, meaning it was continually repopulated with the sweetest things of life.

All the Israelites had to do was trust in God's promises to claim this good and spacious land flowing with milk and honey. But, as we saw in the incident with the golden calf, the people were quick to doubt God's word and turn back to the idols they had served in Egypt. Even though the Lord had set them free, they were still living as slaves. Yet even in spite of their rebellion, the Lord did not draw back his promise of giving them the land:

> [1] *Then the Lord said to Moses, "Leave this place, you and the people you brought up out of Egypt, and go up to the land I promised on oath to Abraham, Isaac and Jacob, saying, 'I will give it to your descendants.' [2] I will send an angel before you and drive out the Canaanites, Amorites, Hittites, Perizzites, Hivites and Jebusites. [3] Go up to the land flowing with milk and honey. But I will not go with you, because you are a stiff-necked people and I might destroy you on the way." . . .*
>
> [12] *Moses said to the Lord, "You have been telling me, 'Lead these people,' but you have not let me know whom you will send with me. You have said, 'I know*

you by name and you have found favor with me.' ¹³ If you are pleased with me, teach me your ways so I may know you and continue to find favor with you. Remember that this nation is your people."

¹⁴ The LORD replied, "My Presence will go with you, and I will give you rest."

¹⁵ Then Moses said to him, "If your Presence does not go with us, do not send us up from here. ¹⁶ How will anyone know that you are pleased with me and with your people unless you go with us? What else will distinguish me and your people from all the other people on the face of the earth?"

¹⁷ And the LORD said to Moses, "I will do the very thing you have asked, because I am pleased with you and I know you by name."

Exodus 33:1–3, 12–17

The Lord ultimately showed that he was pleased with his servant Moses by continuing to make his presence known among the people. The Israelites had turned their backs on God, but he would not turn his back on them. Even though they were a "stiff-necked people," he would continue to lead them to the Promised Land.

5. The Israelites had been slaves in Egypt for generations, so it would have been enough for God to just answer their prayers by delivering them. But the Lord went further by stating he would give them the good, spacious, and luxurious land that he had promised to Abraham. When are some times that God likewise exceeded your expectations in the way that he answered your prayers?

6. How did God demonstrate his faithfulness in keeping his promises after the Israelites rebelled at Mount Sinai and worshiped the golden calf?

Consequences for Rebellion

Sadly, even this act of God's grace did not curb the people's rebellious nature. After crossing the wilderness from Egypt, the Israelites arrived at the brink of the Promised Land. Moses sent twelve spies into the region to check it out, and they brought back a report that it was just as God promised: "We went into the land to which you sent us, and it does flow with milk and honey!" (Numbers 13:27). But ten of the spies saw a huge problem. The people already living in the land were powerful—like giants—and the cities were large and fortified. The ten spies concluded, "We can't attack those people; they are stronger than we are" (verse 31).

The Israelites once again did not take God at his word and continued to doubt and rebel. So God, as a righteous judge, reminded his people that sin has consequences. His people were meant to live in the land and worship him as he deserved. But they were unwilling to trust him. Therefore, God decreed, "Not one of those who saw my glory and the signs I performed in Egypt and in the wilderness but who disobeyed me and tested me ten times—not one of them will ever see the land I promised on oath to their ancestors. No one who has treated me with contempt will ever see it" (Numbers 14:22–23).

Ouch! Talk about a punishment. Not even Moses, the leader of the people, would be allowed to enter the Promised Land. Only Joshua and Caleb—the two spies who said the people should trust in God and take the land—would be able to enter. The rest would be made to wander in the wilderness for forty years, "until the whole generation of those who had done evil in his sight was gone" (Numbers 32:13). The people were given what God had promised, but they were too afraid to take the land, so they were not allowed to enter into it.

But God remained gracious and did not abandon them. In fact, the books of Numbers and Deuteronomy recount the way that God cared for his people in the wilderness as he taught them that he could be trusted. Moses demonstrated for the people the reality that "man does not live on bread alone but on every word that comes from the mouth of the LORD" (Deuteronomy 8:3). The forty years in the wilderness was a time for the Israelites to learn humility and teach their children to not make their same mistakes. After those forty years, the Lord appeared to Joshua, who by this time had taken up the mantle of leadership, and told him that it was time to mobilize the Israelites to take the Promised Land.

¹ *After the death of Moses the servant of the LORD, the LORD said to Joshua son of Nun, Moses' aide:* ² *"Moses my servant is dead. Now then, you and all these people, get ready to cross the Jordan River into the land I am about to give to them—to the Israelites.* ³ *I will give you every place where you set your foot, as I promised Moses.* ⁴ *Your territory will extend from the desert to Lebanon, and from the great river, the Euphrates—all the Hittite country—to the Mediterranean Sea in the west.* ⁵ *No one will be able to stand against you all the days of your life. As I was with Moses, so I will be with you; I will never leave you nor forsake you.* ⁶ *Be strong and courageous, because you will lead these people to inherit the land I swore to their ancestors to give them.*

⁷ *"Be strong and very courageous. Be careful to obey all the law my servant Moses gave you; do not turn from it to the right or to the left, that you may be successful wherever you go.* ⁸ *Keep this Book of the Law always on your lips; meditate on it day and night, so that you may be careful to do everything written in it. Then you will be prosperous and successful.* ⁹ *Have I not commanded you? Be strong and courageous. Do not be afraid; do not be discouraged, for the LORD your God will be with you wherever you go."*

¹⁰ *So Joshua ordered the officers of the people:* ¹¹ *"Go through the camp and tell the people, 'Get your provisions ready. Three days from now you will cross*

*the Jordan here to go in and take possession of the land the L*ORD *your God is giving you for your own.'"*

Joshua 1:1–11

The stories throughout the book of Joshua reveal one common theme: it is God who fights on behalf of his people. The Israelites take the land because God is faithful to his promise, not because the people are strong, powerful, or numerous. The battle of Jericho in Joshua 5–6 is a vivid picture of this reality—one scene of many in which God shows off his might.

The inhabitants of the land were strong and worshiped all sorts of gods other than the one true God. The Lord told Israel they must drive them out or else they would never experience true rest. They would always be fighting with someone. Furthermore, if the pagan nations were right at their doorstep, given enough time, the Israelites would surely succumb to worshiping false gods as well. Jericho proved that if the people would trust in God, they would be able to conquer anyone. They had nothing to fear as long as their faith was in God and his promises.

7. Why would Joshua, and the nation of Israel, need to be strong and courageous?

8. What did God say the people needed to do to be prosperous and successful?

REFLECT

No one in their right mind would have devised a military strategy in which the fighting men put away their swords and just marched around the city led by priests. When we read the battle plan in today's context, we have to wonder what the Israelites thought about it. They did not try take the city by force, as would have been common for all conquests in that day. Rather, they took the city by faith. They trusted God's word, did what he said, and watched him display his might. This would serve as the path to victory for Israel in other battles.

But God also had something else in mind with the land. He wasn't simply out to give his people a great place to call home—though the land would certainly be that. He also wanted to set his people up so they could radiate his glory. God knew the Promised Land would be a prime place for his people to impact the world. Because of its location and bountiful provision, the surrounding nations would be regularly drawn to the Promised Land. People would see God worshiped in the temple, a permanent house akin to the tabernacle used in the wilderness. They would also see God's people live in harmony with him as they obeyed his laws.

Furthermore, society would function as it should because people would love their neighbors as themselves. And through the sacrificial system, people would understand that God's holiness and human sin could not coexist. The onlooking nations would see their need for a sacrificial substitute. As God said through the prophet Isaiah, "I will also make you a light for the Gentiles, that my salvation may reach to the ends of the earth" (Isaiah 49:6). God was after what he had always been after—for his people to reflect his glory so the entire world would know his greatness—and wanted to use Israel to do just that from the Promised Land.

9. What was God teaching his people at the conquest of Jericho?

10. What did God intend his people to do once they were in the Promised Land?

CLOSE

Israel would prove to be woefully inadequate in this mission. As we will see in the next lesson, they did not learn from their experience in the wilderness—at least not for long. They were unable, or unwilling, to live as lights to the other peoples around them. An entire nation, equipped with everything they needed for success, failed at God's mission to live as light. So, thousands of years later, God did something dramatic. He didn't raise up another nation to take Israel's place; rather, he sent a singular person to live as the light. As John's Gospel says, "The true light that gives light to everyone was coming into the world" (John 1:9).

This light—Jesus Christ—came so the world could witness the glory of God (see verse 14). He did what Israel failed to do, and he did it in a most unusual way. God came in the flesh—100-percent God and 100-percent man—to this earth. He came to our place—a place infested by human sin and brokenness. The Light came to our darkness so we could know the Light. His love invades our places—our homes, apartments, dorm rooms. Places we love. Even those we hate. He makes his dwelling among us and promises those of us who love him a future home that will make the Promised Land pale in comparison. He has gone to prepare a place for all God's children, and one day he will come back and take us to his place forever (John 14:3).

11. Why was the Israelites' forty years in the wilderness necessary? In what ways have you experienced a wilderness in your life?

12. How is the Promised Land a picture of Jesus?

EXILE

The people returned to ways even more correct than those of their ancestors. . . . They refused to give up their evil practices and stubborn ways.

JUDGES 2:19

He is patient with you, not wanting anyone to perish, but everyone to come to repentance.

2 PETER 3:9

God will bring every

deed into

judgment . . . whether

it is good or evil.

— ECCLESIASTES 12:14

WELCOME

Some clichés are spoken so frequently in today's society that many people assume them to be universal laws. "Opposites attract." "Laughter is the best medicine." "The grass is always greener on the other side." These maxims are used as short-hand ways of referring to realities that are often the case. The story of Israel, as told in the Old Testament, can also be summarized in a concise cliché: "If something seems too good to be true, it probably is."

Throughout this study, we have followed the course of the Israelites up to their conquest of the Promised Land. The people had been chosen by God and promised his love through a covenant with Abraham (Genesis). They had been miraculously rescued from slavery in Egypt under Moses and given God's Law, so they knew how to live (Exodus). God then introduced the sacrificial system so sinful people could have a way to worship him (Leviticus). Even though they had rebelled and failed to trust in God, the Israelites had been protected during their years in the wilderness (Numbers) and learned to depend on God as their only hope for life (Deuteronomy). Finally, they were ready to take the Promised Land, which they did with the power and might of God (Joshua).

But, as we will soon see, it was too good to be true.

Judges opens with hints to this truth: "When Israel became strong, they pressed the Canaanites into forced labor but never drove them out completely" (Judges 1:28). Again and again, we see the tribes of Israel failing in their mission to rid the Promised Land of the pagan nations and instead allowing them to remain. Just as God promised, the constant threat of warfare and the worship of foreign gods that resulted soon began to destroy Israel.

1. What are some too-good-to-be-true moments that you've experienced in life?

2. Why do you think it's so easy to not trust in God as much when things are going well?

READ

Playing by Your Own Rules

The Israelites remained true to the Lord as long as Joshua was alive to lead them. But after his death, "another generation grew up who knew neither the Lord nor what he had done for Israel . . . [they] did evil in the eyes of the Lord" (Judges 2:10–11). So God removed his hand of protection and allowed foreign powers to invade. When the people cried out to God in their distress, he raised up human leaders, known as judges, who prodded the people back toward faithfulness. This passage in Judges reveals the pattern that would occur for centuries:

¹² They forsook the LORD, the God of their ancestors, who had brought them out of Egypt. They followed and worshiped various gods of the peoples around them. They aroused the LORD's anger ¹³ because they forsook him and served Baal and the Ashtoreths. ¹⁴ In his anger against Israel the LORD gave them into the hands of raiders who plundered them. He sold them into the hands of their enemies all around, whom they were no longer able to resist. ¹⁵ Whenever Israel went out to fight, the hand of the LORD was against them to defeat them, just as he had sworn to them. They were in great distress.

¹⁶ Then the LORD raised up judges, who saved them out of the hands of these raiders. ¹⁷ Yet they would not listen to their judges but prostituted themselves to other gods and worshiped them. They quickly turned from the ways of their ancestors, who had been obedient to the LORD's commands. ¹⁸ Whenever the LORD raised up a judge for them, he was with the judge and saved them out of the hands of their enemies as long as the judge lived; for the LORD relented because of their groaning under those who oppressed and afflicted them. ¹⁹ But when the judge died, the people returned to ways even more corrupt than those of their ancestors, following other gods and serving and worshiping them. They refused to give up their evil practices and stubborn ways.

²⁰ Therefore the LORD was very angry with Israel and said, "Because this nation has violated the covenant I ordained for their ancestors and has not listened to me, ²¹ I will no longer drive out before them any of the nations Joshua left when he died. ²² I will use them to test Israel and see whether they will keep the way of the LORD and walk in it as their ancestors did."

Judges 2:12-22

The book of Judges casts an ominous shadow over what is to follow by stating "everyone did as they saw fit" rather than submitting to God's rule (Judges 21:25). The people were finally in the land as God had promised. But it was all too good to be true.

Life never goes well when people do whatever they want. If our desires were perfect, then we could follow our passions and get good results. But the Bible is clear that our desires have been tainted by sin. What we want—our human desires—is generally not in line with what God wants. We are often led astray by the lusts of our flesh. When we do what we want, it only leads to destruction, bondage, and death.

People prove every day that no amount of human pleasure, success, or money can provide ultimate meaning to life. In fact, having an abundance of possessions on this earth often only leads to greater emptiness. You have likely witnessed this in your life—either with those close to you or in your own circumstances—for the pursuit of earthly treasures apart from God's will never ends well. People get what they want only to find that it is too good to be true. Having everything proves to be empty and void of meaning and purpose.

3. What is the typical outcome when everyone just does what they want?

4. Have you seen the pursuit of pleasure, success, or money lead to emptiness? If so, what did that look like?

A Desire for a King

The continued restlessness of the Israelites led them to conclude their problem was that they lacked a king—just like all the other nations had at that time (see 1 Samuel 8:5). It's noteworthy that the people did not accept personal responsibility for their problems. They should have acknowledged that the predicaments they faced were the direct result of their failure and unwillingness to submit to God as their king. But instead, they tried to find a human answer to their spiritual problem. The prophet

Samuel warned the people what would happen if they had a king, but they didn't listen. So God agreed to give the people what they wanted.

6 But when they said, "Give us a king to lead us," this displeased Samuel; so he prayed to the LORD. 7 And the LORD told him: "Listen to all that the people are saying to you; it is not you they have rejected, but they have rejected me as their king. 8 As they have done from the day I brought them up out of Egypt until this day, forsaking me and serving other gods, so they are doing to you. 9 Now listen to them; but warn them solemnly and let them know what the king who will reign over them will claim as his rights."

10 Samuel told all the words of the LORD to the people who were asking him for a king. 11 He said, "This is what the king who will reign over you will claim as his rights: He will take your sons and make them serve with his chariots and horses, and they will run in front of his chariots. 12 Some he will assign to be commanders of thousands and commanders of fifties, and others to plow his ground and reap his harvest, and still others to make weapons of war and equipment for his chariots. 13 He will take your daughters to be perfumers and cooks and bakers. 14 He will take the best of your fields and vineyards and olive groves and give them to his attendants. 15 He will take a tenth of your grain and of your vintage and give it to his officials and attendants. 16 Your male and female servants and the best of your cattle and donkeys he will take for his own use. 17 He will take a tenth of your flocks, and you yourselves will become his slaves. 18 When that day comes, you will cry out for relief from the king you have chosen, but the LORD will not answer you in that day."

19 But the people refused to listen to Samuel. "No!" they said. "We want a king over us. 20 Then we will be like all the other nations, with a king to lead us and to go out before us and fight our battles."

21 When Samuel heard all that the people said, he repeated it before the LORD. 22 The LORD answered, "Listen to them and give them a king."

1 Samuel 8:6–22

The most famous kings in Israel—Saul, David, and Solomon—were used by God to do good in their day, but their own sin hindered their ability to lead the people perfectly in God's ways. Each subsequent king would generally prove incapable of ushering in the peace, prosperity, and rest for which the people longed. Their stories are told primarily in the books of 1 and 2 Samuel, 1 and 2 Kings, and 1 and 2 Chronicles. There were great moments in these historical books—Saul established the nation, David defeated Goliath, Solomon built the temple. But each high point was met by a corresponding low—Saul's perversion of power, David's foray into adultery and murder, and Solomon's proclivity to marry many women from outside of Israel.

5. God gave the people a king, just as they had requested. But in what ways did that "solution" not measure up to solving the people's problems?

6. When was a time in your life where you thought you had a good solution to a problem—only to discover that it was actually not a good solution?

The Road to Exile

After the reign of King Solomon, the nation of Israel split into two parts. The ten northern tribes— Asher, Dan, Ephraim, Gad, Issachar, Manasseh, Nephtali, Reuben, Simeon, and Zebulun—became the kingdom of Israel, while the two southern tribes— Judah and Benjamin—became the kingdom of Judah. None of the nineteen kings who reigned after Solomon in the kingdom of Israel could be considered godly. Only eight of the thirty-nine kings who reigned in Judah—Asa, Jehoshaphat, Joash, Amaziah, Azariah, Jotham, Hezekiah, and Josiah—were noted in Scripture as godly.

Overall, the majority of the kings of both nations led the people into idolatry.

As each king rose to power and failed to lead the people in God's ways, it became clear that the answer the people needed would have to come in another form. God would have to provide a better king, which he would ultimately do by sending them Jesus, the King of kings and Lord of lords. The sign that the Roman soldiers mockingly posted over Jesus' dying body on the cross attested to the truth—"THIS IS JESUS, THE KING OF THE JEWS" (Matthew 27:37). Jesus was the King of the Jews, and he was also the King of the entire world.

Before Jesus arrived, however, the nation of Israel would have to face the just judgment of God for their ongoing rebellion. The Lord had warned that this day would come if they persisted in their waywardness once they were in the Promised Land: "If your heart turns away and you are not obedient, and if you are drawn away to bow down to other gods and worship them, I declare to you this day that you will certainly be destroyed. You will not live long in the land you are crossing the Jordan to enter and possess" (Deuteronomy 30:17–18).

Eventually, the people were kicked out of the land that God had so graciously given to them. This came in the form of conquest by two world powers. First, the kingdom of Israel was captured by the Assyrians in 722 BC. Then, the kingdom of Judah was captured by the Babylonians in 587 BC. The destruction of Jerusalem, with its temple built by Solomon, was the final sign that God was faithful to his promise to judge his persistently wayward people.

1 So in the ninth year of Zedekiah's reign, on the tenth day of the tenth month, Nebuchadnezzar king of Babylon marched against Jerusalem with his whole army. He encamped outside the city and built siege works all around it. 2 The city was kept under siege until the eleventh year of King Zedekiah.

3 By the ninth day of the fourth month the famine in the city had become so severe that there was no food for the people to eat. 4 Then the city wall was broken through, and the whole army fled at night through the gate between the two walls near the king's garden, though the Babylonians were surrounding the city. They fled toward the Arabah, 5 but the Babylonian army pursued the king and overtook him in the plains of Jericho. All his soldiers were separated from him and scattered, 6 and he was captured.

He was taken to the king of Babylon at Riblah, where sentence was pronounced on him. ⁷ They killed the sons of Zedekiah before his eyes. Then they put out his eyes, bound him with bronze shackles and took him to Babylon.

⁸ On the seventh day of the fifth month, in the nineteenth year of Nebuchadnezzar king of Babylon, Nebuzaradan commander of the imperial guard, an official of the king of Babylon, came to Jerusalem. ⁹ He set fire to the temple of the LORD, the royal palace and all the houses of Jerusalem. Every important building he burned down. ¹⁰ The whole Babylonian army under the commander of the imperial guard broke down the walls around Jerusalem. ¹¹ Nebuzaradan the commander of the guard carried into exile the people who remained in the city, along with the rest of the populace and those who had deserted to the king of Babylon.

2 Kings 25:1–11

The Lord had been slow in enacting his judgment, proving himself to be a God who was slow to anger and abounding in steadfast love. Time and time again, he gave his people space to repent from their sins and walk faithfully with him. The apostle Peter, writing much later, said the same is true even today. God has promised that Jesus will return, and when he does, he will judge those who haven't placed their faith in him for salvation. They will face God's eternal wrath. But God delays—not because he doesn't hate sin, but because he is patient with people, "not wanting anyone to perish, but everyone to come to repentance" (2 Peter 3:9).

7. In what ways was the Lord patient with the people of Israel and Judah?

8. How have you witnessed God's patience on display in your life?

REFLECT

It would be a mistake to understand God's patience as a license to sin, as if God is somehow unconcerned or unwilling to judge sinners. Rather, God's forbearance and patience is meant to lead people to repentance (see Romans 2:4). God gives those he loves time to admit their sin and humble themselves before him. This kindness is extended to everyone—even those who have turned their backs on God and mocked his name. Each breath we take is evidence of God's incredible patience with us. How we respond to that act of kindness is our choice.

The nation of Israel chose death. Like Adam and Eve before them, the people of God proved incapable of keeping God's law and had to be banished from the land of God's blessing. The Israelites who survived the conquests were exiled to foreign lands—a far cry from God's holy people living in his Promised Land and radiating his glory to the watching world.

People today experience a hint of these consequences when they find themselves broken under the weight of their sin. It's common to hear people speak of "hitting rock bottom"—a point in their lives when their poor choices have led them to such brokenness and pain that they have no one to turn to but God. This process is yet another indication of God's love. Sometimes he lets our sin run its course. In the words of Paul, "God gives them over in the sinful desires of their hearts" (Romans 1:24). When we live apart from God, the depths of the despair we experience should bring us to our senses and cause us to come back to him.

Jesus spoke about this in one of his most famous stories—the parable of the prodigal son. This prodigal son asked for his inheritance, left home, and spent all of his money on wild living. He did whatever he wanted and in return got what he deserved for his sin. He came to the end of himself when he was so famished that he wanted to eat the food that he fed to the pigs. This caused him to return home to his father, who was waiting with arms outstretched in love (see Luke 15:11–32). God, the father in this story, was patient with his youngest boy even when that son wanted nothing to do with him. God allowed the young man to experience the consequences of his sin, which humbled him and brough him back to the Father.

This is just what God wants to do with you. He wants your sin to break you so you see that you have no other hope except for the salvation he offers. Humility is the place where faith begins. You come undone in your brokenness and fling yourself on God's mercy. When you do, you experience the Father's love in unimaginable ways in spite of the mess you have made.

9. Why does God choose to be patient with people today who sin against him?

10. What does the parable of the prodigal son reveal about God's heart for us?

CLOSE

In the ongoing life of a Christian, we still sin, and God still offers his grace. We may try to mask our sin, hide it from others and from God, or pretend that it doesn't exist.

But when we come clean and admit our need for God's grace and deliverance, we find true freedom.

This is all because of Jesus. The author of Hebrews tells us that Jesus provides the true rest that the people of Israel longed for and that we still need today (see Hebrews 4:1–11). He provides rest from the oppressive weight of our sin and rest from the excruciating pain of knowing that we don't add up. Jesus frees us from all of that. He knows our sin, personally. He bore our sin on the cross. He paid its penalty.

So when we come to him in faith, we experience the type of rest the Promised Land was meant to provide but never did. We find love, joy, peace, and wholeness. The weary and heavy-laden come to him and find that his yoke is easy and his burden is light (see Matthew 11:28–30). Jesus gives rest to those who humble themselves and admit they need it.

11. What impact has God's kindness and patience had on you in the way you think and act?

12. In what areas of your life do you still need to experience God's promise of rest?

SCRIPTURE

"I will put my Spirit in you and you will live, and I will settle you in your own land. Then you will know that I the LORD have spoken, and I have done it, declares the LORD."

EZEKIEL 37:14

"This is my blood of the covenant, which is poured out for many for the forgiveness of sins."

MATTHEW 26:28

The grass withers . . .
but the word
of our God
endures forever.

— ISAIAH 40:8

WELCOME

For a moment, imagine you are waiting on a plane, ready to take off. At first, the momentary delays barely register because you are stowing your bags, finding your headphones, and getting settled into your seat. The boarding passengers stream by you and, in time, the cabin door closes as the crew prepares for departure. But the plane doesn't move. You continue to sit in the cramped space, waiting for the plane to be pushed back from the gate.

As minutes pass and the plane sits idle, you look at your watch and start to think about the plans you have waiting for you at your destination. But thirty minutes later, still nothing has happened. By now you notice other passengers talking to each another, trying to figure out what is causing the delay. In the commotion, the captain finally speaks: "Ladies and gentlemen, I am sorry for the delay . . ."

Regardless of the words that follow, the captain's voice is a welcome respite to the uncertainty of the moment. His words remind you that there is someone in charge of the plane—a person monitoring the situation and determining the best course of action for everyone who is onboard. If the captain never spoke—if he or she only opened the cabin doors after the mandated time to allow the passengers to "egress" according to the rules—then only confusion and anarchy would ensue. People simply cannot deal with uncertainty for very long.

1. When is a time that someone spoke into your life in a way that brought comfort?

2. What was it about this person that made you trust him or her?

READ

God's Voice in Uncertainty

Uncertainty surely plagued the people of Israel during the exile. Gone were the days of peace and prosperity. Now God's people lived in pagan nations, with only memories of the land flowing with milk and honey. Some likely felt regret as they reflected on the times in their history when they could have turned to God and avoided this fate. Some certainly caved to the pressures of living in a foreign world and acted as if the one true God did not exist. Most of the people probably felt an overwhelming sense of fear and dread as they thought about the future. Had God finally given up on them? Was there any hope? Into this uncertainly the Lord sent prophets like Eze-kiel to let his people know that he had not forgotten them:

¹ The hand of the LORD was on me, and he brought me out by the Spirit of the LORD and set me in the middle of a valley; it was full of bones. ² He led me back and forth among them, and I saw a great many bones on the floor of the valley, bones that were very dry. ³ He asked me, "Son of man, can these bones live?"

I said, "Sovereign LORD, you alone know."

⁴ Then he said to me, "Prophesy to these bones and say to them, 'Dry bones, hear the word of the LORD! ⁵ This is what the Sovereign LORD says to these bones: I will make breath enter you, and you will come to life. ⁶ I will attach tendons to you and make flesh come upon you and cover you with skin; I will put breath in you, and you will come to life. Then you will know that I am the LORD.'"

⁷ So I prophesied as I was commanded. And as I was prophesying, there was a noise, a rattling sound, and the bones came together, bone to bone. ⁸ I looked, and tendons and flesh appeared on them and skin covered them, but there was no breath in them.

⁹ Then he said to me, "Prophesy to the breath; prophesy, son of man, and say to it, 'This is what the Sovereign LORD says: Come, breath, from the four winds and breathe into these slain, that they may live.'" ¹⁰ So I prophesied as he commanded me, and breath entered them; they came to life and stood up on their feet—a vast army.

¹¹ Then he said to me: "Son of man, these bones are the people of Israel. They say, 'Our bones are dried up and our hope is gone; we are cut off.' ¹² Therefore prophesy and say to them: 'This is what the Sovereign LORD says: My people, I am going to open your graves and bring you up from them; I will bring you back to the land of Israel. ¹³ Then you, my people, will know that I am the LORD, when I open your graves and bring you up from them. ¹⁴ I will put my Spirit in you and you will live, and I will settle you in your own land. Then you will know that I the LORD have spoken, and I have done it, declares the LORD.'"

Ezekiel 37:1–14

In this time of instability, the people of Israel needed to hear the voice of their "captain"—and the Lord spoke to them. Think about this for a moment. God did not have to speak. He would have been perfectly within his rights to keep quiet and force the nation to figure it out on their own. He had already given them so much guidance. They had his law, which instructed them how to love him and love others. They had wisdom from the greats like David and Solomon, which taught them about the practical aspects of following God in this world. They had beautiful songs of praise that captured the essence of God's character and His faithful love. God had spoken, and the people had failed to listen. He did not have to say anything else.

But he did.

3. When is a time that you wondered if God had turned his back on you?

4. How did God ultimately reveal his presence to you in that situation?

The Role of the Prophets

God often chose to speak to his people—both before, during, and after the exile—through his prophets. These individuals wrote down God's words in the books that generally bear their names. In total, they represent the final seventeen books of the

Old Testament. Five of these books—Isaiah, Jeremiah, Lamentations (believed to have been written by Jeremiah), Ezekiel, and Daniel—are referred to as the "Major Prophets." The remaining twelve books—Hosea, Joel, Amos, Obadiah, Jonah, Micah, Nahum, Habakkuk, Zephaniah, Haggai, Zechariah, and Malachi—are often called the "Minor Prophets."

It is important to note here that the "major" and "minor" designation has nothing to do with importance of each prophet's message. Rather, the terms distinguish those books that are longer (major) from those that are shorter (minor). The prophets had a unified task—to speak to God's people on God's behalf. As far back as Moses, we observe God using human beings to speak his words to those who needed it the most. He still does this today through pastors and leaders who have the task of echoing God's words to the church. Like the prophets, they have the role of ensuring that their words rightly reflect God's words.

As noted previously, the Old Testament prophets spoke to the people of Israel at different stages of their journey. Some wrote before the exile. Their voices were of warning—that God would judge the people if they did not repent of their sin and turn back to him. Some wrote during the exile. Their voices testified of God's faithfulness to his people and urged those in exile to trust in his future restoration. Some wrote after the exile, when the nation began to return back to Jerusalem. Their voices urged the remaining Israelites to learn the lessons the exile had taught them and to be true to God during this stage of their nation's history.

> ¹ *Do not rejoice, Israel;*
> *do not be jubilant like the other nations.*
> *For you have been unfaithful to your God;*
> *you love the wages of a prostitute*
> *at every threshing floor.*
> ² *Threshing floors and winepresses will not feed the people;*
> *the new wine will fail them.*
> ³ *They will not remain in the Lord's land;*
> *Ephraim will return to Egypt*
> *and eat unclean food in Assyria.*
>
> Hosea 9:1–3 (before the exile)

*14 The word of the L*ORD *came to me: 15 "Son of man, the people of Jerusalem have said of your fellow exiles and all the other Israelites, 'They are far away from the L*ORD*; this land was given to us as our possession.'*

*16 "Therefore say: 'This is what the Sovereign L*ORD *says: Although I sent them far away among the nations and scattered them among the countries, yet for a little while I have been a sanctuary for them in the countries where they have gone.'*

*17 "Therefore say: 'This is what the Sovereign L*ORD *says: I will gather you from the nations and bring you back from the countries where you have been scattered, and I will give you back the land of Israel again.'"*

Ezekiel 11:14–17 (during the exile)

*2 "The L*ORD *was very angry with your ancestors. 3 Therefore tell the people: This is what the L*ORD *Almighty says: 'Return to me,' declares the L*ORD *Almighty, 'and I will return to you,' says the L*ORD *Almighty. 4 Do not be like your ancestors, to whom the earlier prophets proclaimed: This is what the L*ORD *Almighty says: 'Turn from your evil ways and your evil practices.' But they would not listen or pay attention to me, declares the L*ORD*. 5 Where are your ancestors now? And the prophets, do they live forever? 6 But did not my words and my decrees, which I commanded my servants the prophets, overtake your ancestors?'"*

Zechariah 1:2–6 (after the exile)

You might expect that God's voice to his people would have been akin to that of parents who have told their toddlers again and again to not touch a hot stove. When the children fail to listen and burn their hands, the parents respond with an "I told you so!" God the Father had warned his people of the threat of the exile. He had told them it was coming. He had even revealed many of the exact details of the exile long before it happened, including the nations he would use to crush to enact his judgment. God could have said, "I told you so!"

Certainly, the prophets do testify that the Israelites are facing the direct consequences of their foolish choices. But there is also a message of hope, redemption, and restoration in God's words. The prophet Ezekiel, as noted previously, pictures the people as a valley of dry bones that come to life at God's commands. The assertion is that if the Lord can raise up dead bones, he surely is capable of restoring the fortunes of Israel. In a similar tone, the prophet Isaiah wrote, "Comfort, comfort my people, says your God. Speak tenderly to Jerusalem" (Isaiah 40:1–2). *Comfort into chaos.* This is the word of the Lord to his people.

How could such a tender, compassionate, caring word be spoken to a people who had demonstrated nothing but stiff-necked rebellion? The answer is simple: God's word is based on his character and his covenant promises. He would prove faithful to the people and restore them, not because of any merit in them, but because he is always faithful to the commitments he makes. He pledged his love to the people. He promised to be their God, and they his people.

Nothing, not even their ongoing sin, could usurp God's good promises. Isaiah reinforced this truth when he wrote, "The Lord says—he who formed me in the womb to be his servant to bring Jacob back to him and gather Israel to himself, for I am honored in the eyes of the Lord and my God has been my strength—he says: 'It is too small a thing for you to be my servant to restore the tribes of Jacob and bring back those of Israel I have kept. I will also make you a light for the Gentiles, that my salvation may reach to the ends of the earth' ' (Isaiah 49:5–6).

5. Have you ever heard "I told you so" from someone? How did it make you feel?

6. When is a time you should have heard "I told you so" from someone—but instead you received a gracious response? How did that make you feel?

The Only Hope Is a Savior

These promises from God were messages of hope to the returning exiles. But one can't help but wonder if the people would just go right back to where they started once they had resettled into the land. God had saved his people before. He had restored their fortunes and given them his blessing. Now that he was doing it again for them after the return from exile, wouldn't it only be a matter of time before the people were wallowing in sin once more? The prophets answered this question by pointing to something unique that God was about to do.

> ³¹ *"The days are coming," declares the LORD,*
>   *"when I will make a new covenant*
> *with the people of Israel*
>   *and with the people of Judah.*
> ³² *It will not be like the covenant*
>   *I made with their ancestors*
> *when I took them by the hand*
>   *to lead them out of Egypt,*
> *because they broke my covenant,*
>   *though I was a husband to them,"*
>   *declares the LORD.*
> ³³ *"This is the covenant I will make with the people of Israel*
>   *after that time," declares the LORD.*
> *"I will put my law in their minds*
>   *and write it on their hearts.*
> *I will be their God,*
>   *and they will be my people.*

34 *No longer will they teach their neighbor,*
   or say to one another, 'Know the LORD,'
because they will all know me,
   from the least of them to the greatest,"
   declares the LORD.
"For I will forgive their wickedness
   and will remember their sins no more."

Jeremiah 31:31–34

2 *He grew up before him like a tender shoot,*
   and like a root out of dry ground.
He had no beauty or majesty to attract us to him,
   nothing in his appearance that we should desire him.
3 *He was despised and rejected by mankind,*
   a man of suffering, and familiar with pain.
Like one from whom people hide their faces
   he was despised, and we held him in low esteem.
4 *Surely he took up our pain*
   and bore our suffering,
yet we considered him punished by God,
   stricken by him, and afflicted.
5 *But he was pierced for our transgressions,*
   he was crushed for our iniquities;
the punishment that brought us peace was on him,
   and by his wounds we are healed.
6 *We all, like sheep, have gone astray,*
   each of us has turned to our own way;
and the LORD has laid on him
   the iniquity of us all.

Isaiah 53:2–6

God promises a new covenant with his people—not one that is different from the covenant he made with Israel, but one that makes possible the realization of those covenant promises. God pledges to save his people and write his law on their hearts. This covenant will not depend on outward conformity to the law but will be an inner salvation that God will accomplish for his people. He will then send his Spirit to fill those he saves and give them the desire and power to worship the Lord as he deserves.

Isaiah provides a startling vision for how this will be accomplished. The promised Savior, the one pictured all the way back in Genesis 3, will lay down his life as a substitute for the sins of the people. He will offer his life as a sacrifice, holy and acceptable to God, and this sacrifice will fully and finally satisfy the wrath of God for the sins of the people. At the end of the Old Testament, Israel would have understood that their only hope rested in God sending a Savior!

7. What promise is given in Jeremiah 31:31–34? What is unique about this promise?

8. How is Isaiah 53:2–6 a picture of Jesus? What will he do for the people?

REFLECT

It would have been difficult for the returning exiles to imagine the beauty of Christ and the way he would fulfill these promises. But looking back, we can see that God had a plan for his people, and he has never stopped working out that plan to perfect completion. From our vantage point, the promises of God delivered through the prophets make sense.

Even during New Testament times, it was still hard for the early followers of Jesus to grasp the extent of his work and the way he would fulfill all the promises and patterns set out in the Old Testament. Imagine the disciples' shock when Jesus broke the bread and poured out the wine at the Passover meal shortly before his death and declared: "This is my blood of the covenant, which is poured out for many for the forgiveness of sins" (Matthew 26:28).

Jesus' coming death was the fulfillment of the promises of God throughout the Old Testament. He was the Seed of Eve who would crush the serpent's head. He was the Lamb of God who would take away the sins of the world. He was the Son of God who would perfectly keep God's law in his thoughts and actions. He was the temple, the dwelling place of God with his people. He was the great High Priest, the mediator between God and sinful humanity. He was the Word made flesh, the fulfillment of the hope of the people since Adam and Eve's first sin.

9. What role did the prophets play in God's story? What did they tell the people of Israel about the past, present, and future?

10. How does the story of the Israelites encourage you in your faith?

CLOSE

Jesus is the one who makes sense of the Bible. He is the key to understanding the story that God is writing in this world. All of the themes, pictures, stories, and images find fulfillment in Christ. Scripture isn't merely a collection of truths for how to live a good life. Rather, it is a testimony that the good life is impossible unless God acts to save sinners from themselves. Jesus is the hope of a sinful people living in a sin-drenched world.

11. What big ideas from *People* have stuck with you? How have these truths changed the way you think about yourself, your community, and God?

12. What do you sense that God has been saying to you as you've gone through this study?

NEXT

Throughout these six lessons of *People,* we have seen how God was always faithful to his people and kept his promises to them in spite of their many failings. We have explored how God, through a man named Abraham, commissioned a chosen people to be a witness of his faithfulness on earth. We saw that even though these chosen people rejected God time and again, the Lord was always gracious and showed them mercy when they repented and called on his name. Most important, we discovered that at each turn of his people's cycle of rejection, repentance, and restoration, the Lord continued to move forward and announce his plan of salvation for the world.

In *Savior,* the next study in the *Jesus Bible Study Series,* we will be introduced to the hero of God's story—Jesus, the only Son of God, who would bring God's plan of redemption to fulfillment. In the fullness of time, this promised Savior was born in a humble stable to humble earthly parents in the city of Bethlehem. Jesus brought an end to the system of sacrifice and ritual. Once and for all, he appeased God's wrath through his death on the cross, opening the way for rebels to come home to a peace-making Father. Now, all come to the Father through him.

Thank you for taking this journey! Stay the course. God has a lot that he wants to do in your life!

LEADER'S GUIDE

Thank you for your willingness to lead your group through this study. What you have chosen to do is valuable and will make a great difference in the lives of others. The rewards of being a leader are different from those of participating, and we hope that as you lead you will find your own walk with Jesus deepened by the experience.

The lessons in this study guide are suitable for church classes, Bible studies, and small groups. Each lesson is structured to provoke thought and help you grow in your knowledge and understanding of Christ. There are multiple components in this section that can help you structure your lessons and discussion time, so make sure you read and consider each one.

BEFORE YOU BEGIN

Before your first meeting, make sure the group members have a copy of this study guide so they can follow along and have their answers written out ahead of time. Alternately, you can hand out the study guides at your first meeting and give the group members some time to look over the material and ask any preliminary questions. During your first meeting, be sure to send a sheet of paper around the room and have the members write down their name, phone number, and email address so you can keep in touch with them during the week.

Generally, the ideal size for a group is eight to ten people, which will ensure that everyone has enough time to participate in discussions. If you have more people, you might want to break up the main group into smaller subgroups. Encourage those who show up at the first meeting to commit to attending the duration of the study. This will help the group members get to know one another, create stability for the group, and help you, as the leader, know how to best prepare each week.

Try to initiate a free-flowing discussion as you go through each lesson. Invite group members to bring any questions they have or insights they discover as they go through the content to the next meeting, especially if they were unsure of the meaning of some parts of the lesson. Be prepared to discuss the biblical truth that relates to each topic in the study.

WEEKLY PREPARATION

As the group leader, here are a few things you can do to prepare for each meeting:

- Make sure you understand the content of the lesson so you know how to structure group time and are prepared to lead group discussion.
- Depending on how much time you have each week, you may not be able to reflect on every question. Select specific questions that you feel will evoke the best discussion.
- At the end of your discussion, take prayer requests from your group members and pray for each other.

STRUCTURING THE DISCUSSION TIME

It is up to you to keep track of the time and keep things on schedule. You might want to set a timer for each question that you discuss so both you and the group members know when your time is up. (There are some good phone apps for timers that play a gentle chime or other pleasant sound instead of a disruptive noise.)

Don't be concerned if the group members are quiet or slow to share. People are often quiet when they are pulling together their ideas, and this might be a new experience for them. Just ask a question and let it hang in the air until someone shares. You can then say, "Thank you. What about others? What thoughts came to you?"

If you need help in organizing your time when planning your group Bible study, the following schedule, for sixty minutes and ninety minutes, can give you a structure for the lesson:

	60 Minutes	90 Minutes
Welcome: Arrive and get settled	5 minutes	10 minutes
Message: Review the lesson	15 minutes	25 minutes
Discussion: Discuss study questions	35 minutes	45 minutes
Prayer: Pray together and dismiss	5 minutes	10 minutes

GROUP DYNAMICS

Leading a group through *People* will prove to be highly rewarding both to you and your group members. But you still may encounter challenges along the way! Discussions can get off track. Group members may not be sensitive to the needs and ideas of others. Some might worry they will be expected to talk about matters that make them feel awkward. Others may express comments that result in disagreements. To help ease this strain on you and the group, consider the following ground rules:

- When someone raises a question or comment that is off the main topic, suggest you deal with it another time, or, if you feel led to go in that direction, let the group know you will be spending some time discussing it.

- If someone asks a question that you don't know how to answer, admit it and move on. At your discretion, feel free to invite group members to comment on questions that call for personal experience.

- If you find one or two people are dominating the discussion time, direct a few questions to others in the group. Outside the main group time, ask the more dominating members to help you draw out the quieter ones. Work to make them a part of the solution instead of the problem.

- When a disagreement occurs, encourage the group members to process the matter in love. Encourage those on opposite sides to restate what they heard the other side say about the matter, and then invite each side to evaluate if that perception is accurate. Lead the group in examining other Scriptures related to the topic and look for common ground.

When any of these issues arise, encourage your group members to follow these words from the Bible: "Love one another" (John 13:34), "If it is possible, as far as it depends on you, live at peace with everyone" (Romans 12:18), "Whatever is true . . . noble . . . right . . . if anything is excellent or praiseworthy—think about such things" (Philippians 4:8), and "Be quick to listen, slow to speak and slow to become angry" (James 1:19). This will make your group time more rewarding and beneficial for everyone who attends.

Thank you again for your willingness to lead your group. May God reward your efforts and dedication, equip you to guide your group in the weeks ahead, and make your time together in fruitful for his kingdom.

ABOUT THE AUTHORS

Aaron Coe is the founder and CEO of Future City Now, a strategy consulting firm that helps executive leaders maximize their influence on the world. He and his wife, Carmen, have been involved in the Passion Movement for more than twenty years and currently serve as the leaders of the Trilith location of Passion City Church. Aaron has a Ph.D. in Applied Theology and teaches at Dallas Theological Seminary. Additionally, Aaron served as the General Editor of *The Jesus Bible*. Aaron and Carmen live in the Atlanta area with their four children.

Matt Rogers holds a Ph.D. in Applied Theology and teaches and writes on Christian mission, ministry, and discipleship. Notably, Matt served as the lead writer for the bestselling *The Jesus Bible*. He and his wife, Sarah, and their five children live in Greenville, South Carolina, where Matt serves as the pastor of Christ Fellowship Cherrydale.

The Jesus Bible Study Series

Beginnings
ISBN 9780310154983

Revolt
ISBN 9780310155003

People
ISBN 9780310155027

Savior
ISBN 9780310155041

Church
ISBN 9780310155065

Forever
ISBN 9780310155089

Available wherever books are sold

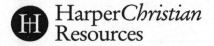

The Jesus Bible

sixty-six books. one story. all about one name.

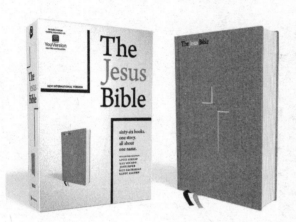

The Jesus Bible, NIV & ESV editions, with feature essays from Louie Giglio, Max Lucado, John Piper, and Randy Alcorn, as well as profound yet accessible study features will help you meet Jesus throughout Scripture.

- 350 full page articles
- 700 side-bar articles
- Book introductions
- Room for journaling

The Jesus Bible Journal, NIV
Study individual books of the Bible featuring lined journal space and commentary from *The Jesus Bible*.

- 14 journals covering 30 books of the Bible
- 2 boxed sets (OT & NT)

TheJesusBible.com

Video Study for Your
Church or Small Group

In this six-session video Bible study, bestselling author and pastor Louie Giglio helps you apply the principles in *Don't Give the Enemy a Seat at Your Table* to your life. The study guide includes access to six streaming video sessions, video notes and a comprehensive structure for group discussion time, and personal study for deeper reflection between sessions.

Study Guide + Streaming Video
9780310156284

DVD
9780310134268

Available now at your favorite bookstore
or streaming video on StudyGateway.com.

It's Not the Height
of the Giant
...but the Size of
Our God

Study Guide + Streaming Video
9780310146506

DVD
9780310083764

EXPLORE THE PRINCIPLES IN *GOLIATH MUST FALL* WITH YOUR small group through this six-session video-based study. Each week, pastor Louie Giglio will provide practical steps and biblical principles for how you and your group can defeat the "giants" in your lives like fear, rejection, comfort, anger, or addiction. Includes discussion questions, Bible exploration, and personal study materials for in between sessions.

 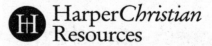